JOHNNY'S EGG

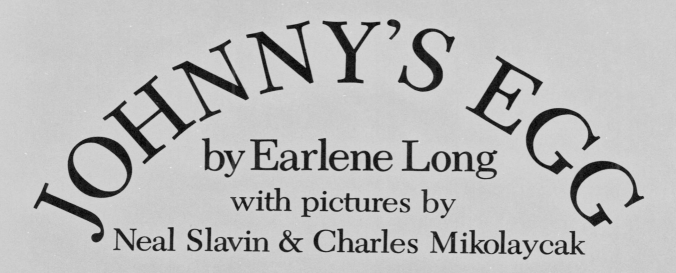

JOHNNY'S EGG

by Earlene Long

with pictures by

Neal Slavin & Charles Mikolaycak

Addison-Wesley

Text Copyright © 1980 by Earlene Long
Pictures Copyright © 1980 by Neal Slavin and Charles Mikolaycak
All Rights Reserved
Addison-Wesley Publishing Company, Inc.
Reading, Massachusetts 01867
Printed in the United States of America

Book designed by Charles Mikolaycak

ABCDEFGHIJK-WZ-89876543210

Library of Congress Cataloging in Publication Data

Long, Earlene, 1938–
Johnny's egg.

SUMMARY: Relates how a little boy successfully breaks
his own egg for breakfast.
[1. Eggs — Fiction. 2. Self-reliance — Fiction]
I. Slavin, Neal. II. Mikolaycak, Charles. III. Title.

PZ7.L8449Jo   [E]   79-21248
ISBN 0-201-04153-7

"Let me," said Johnny. "I want to break my egg."

Mother was in the kitchen making Johnny's breakfast. She looked down at Johnny. His eyes were shining like bright brown marbles.

"Do you think you can break the egg without smashing and squishing all over?" asked his mother.

"I think I can," Johnny said. "Yes, I know I can."

Johnny had tried breaking eggs before. Eggs were hard to break so they didn't smash and squish all over his hands. When he hit the egg too easy, it would not even crack. When he hit the egg too hard, it would make a mess in his hands and drop all over the floor. Today he felt sure he could break the egg without making a mess.

Mother put a small bowl on a stool so Johnny could reach it. She handed him an egg.

Johnny closed his fingers around the egg very carefully. The egg looked very big in Johnny's hand. Johnny felt the egg.

It was very cold and smooth.

He smelled the egg. It didn't smell much.

He felt the egg with the tip of his tongue. The egg was smooth to his tongue but it did not taste much.

Johnny looked up at his mother. She smiled at him. He drew back his hands and hit the egg on the edge of the bowl.

It cracked. He did it. He had hit the egg right in the middle. It didn't smash or squish all over his hand or the floor.

Carefully, Johnny's other hand took hold of the small end of the egg. His face got a closed look as he put his two thumbs at the cracked spot on the egg.

Then Johnny took a deep breath, pushed his thumbs into the crack and pulled them apart.

The egg white and yolk
fell into the little bowl.

"I did it," said Johnny. His face turned pink and seemed to glow. He looked up at his mother. "I broke my very own egg for breakfast."

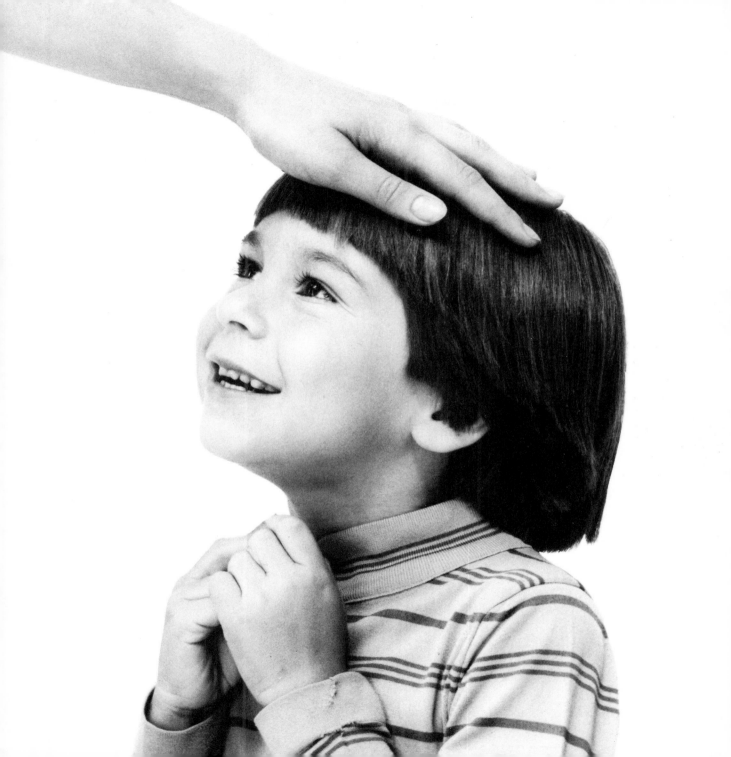

EARLENE LONG received her B.S. in Home Economics from Purdue University. She enjoys reading, stamp and coin collecting, and fishing, but she says, "most of all I enjoy people—in all ways, shapes and being." She has written several stories which have appeared in magazines, but *Johnny's Egg* is her first children's book. Ms. Long lives in Wyoming with her husband and two children, ages 12½ and 9.

CHARLES MIKOLAYCAK is both a book designer and an illustrator whose work has been consistently honored by the American Institute of Graphic Arts. His illustrations for *How The Hare Told The Truth About His Horse* were among those selected to represent the United States at the Bratislava Bienniel of Illustrations. Mr. Mikolaycak has illustrated many children's books, among them *Three Wanderers From Wapping* for Addison-Wesley. He and his wife live in New York City.

NEAL SLAVIN graduated from Cooper Union in New York City and received a scholarship to study Renaissance Painting and Sculpture at Lincoln College, Oxford University in England, a Fulbright Fellowship in Photography to Portugal, and two National Endowment for The Arts grants. In addition to many one-man exhibitions, his works have been included in exhibitions throughout the United States, France and Germany. He has contributed to many publications, has two books to his credit, and has lectured on photography throughout the United States. He was born and still lives in New York City.

JOHNNY'S EGG was designed by Charles Mikolaycak. The type is twenty-four point Caledonia set by Williams Graphic Service, Inc. The book was printed and bound by Worzalla Publishing Company.